THE STAR FISHERMAN

THE STAR FISHERMAN

Robert F. Young

And thine eye shall not pity; but life shall go for life, eye for eye, tooth for tooth, hand for hand, foot for foot. –Deuteronomy 19: 21

Christopher Stark was an "almost" man. He was almost brilliant, he was almost tall, he was almost broad-shouldered, he was almost well-proportioned, and he was almost handsome. His self-image, on the other hand, was everything that he was not.

Now a self-image which is not reasonably in keeping with reality can become a tiger on a man's back. Christopher Stark's tiger clawed him incessantly, and sometimes the pain was too much for him to bear. He could never stop wanting to be something more than what he really was, and he could never stop trying to convince other people that he was something more than what he really was. He convinced quite a few of them in his day, and in the end, when he was dying, he even convinced himself.

When he was twelve years old he boasted to his boyhood sweetheart that someday he would buy himself a shining catamaran and set forth upon the Trans-solar Sea and cast his net into the black deep and snare a thousand fishes for her hair. His boyhood sweetheart eventually married the son of a sausage-maker and became a princess, but Chris, true to his word and true to his tiger, bought his catamaran and set forth and cast his net. Deep-space fishing was an occupation for which he was as ill-suited as he was for winning women, but thanks to his tiger he perfected it to a degree that put potentially greater fishermen to shame. He spurned the berths he could easily have obtained on the innumerable fishing-company trawlers and fished alone, and the catches that he brought in to the Tethys fisheries were tremendous. So were the hangovers that he took back with him to the Trans-solar Sea. As the years passed, he grew more and more contemptuous of his colleagues, and fished in ever deeper waters; and finally one day, in the autumn of his youth, he cast his net and snared a dead man.

Thus his story ended–and thus his story begins.

*

The dead man was drifting in the Alpha Centauri Archipelago some ten million miles from a planet that, in common with its seven sisters, was just as dead as he was. Chris did not snare the body deliberately–he knew nothing of its presence, in fact, until he pulled in his net, and even then he did not recognize the bulky space-suited figure entangled in the magnetic mesh for what it really was. Oftentimes ordinary meteors t raveled with the much smaller, diamond-like variety that men coveted and that women wore in their hair, and it wasn't until after he dragged the net and its contents from the casting deck, through the outer and inner cargo locks and into the brightly illumined hold that he realized the true nature of his catch.

The minute he deactivated the magnetic field, the figure collapsed limply to the deck amid a shower of glittering "fishes." Carefully Chris unscrewed and removed the rime-coated helmet. The face down into which he gazed was the face of an old, old man; and yet, despite its cobwebbed eye-corners, its sunken cheeks and cadaverous complexion, it emanated a swiftly-fading radiance that cast doubt upon the recent death that the rolled-up eyes bespoke. Never-the-less, death had come, and it had come to stay, though whether it had come before or after its victim had been cast adrift in space was a question to which Chris could supply no answer.

He cut away the rest of the suit, revealing an age-shrunken body clad in leisure-class clothing that was much too large for it. Methodically he went through the pockets. They contained no identification of any kind, but they did contain a small roll of blue-backs. He also found a pen, an unwritten-in notebook, and a glossy new photograph. He threw the pen and the notebook away, and pocketed the blue-backs. They would compensate him partly at least for the full catch he had been robbed of. Finally he looked at the photograph.

He was never quite the same afterward.

It was a photograph of a girl. A severe black dress enshrouded her from neck to ankles, and a black bonnet with an immaculate white brim imprisoned her hair . It was an ensemble designed to hide, rather than to enhance, feminine charms, and yet her loveliness flamed forth with a vividness that drove back the gray and brooding shadows of the room in which she stood. Her tawny hair peeped in waves and ringlets from the edges of its bonnet-prison, haloing her face and softening the superimposed sternness of her mouth and chin. The face itself was heart-shaped; the green eyes were wide-apart, as were the Slavic cheekbones. The cheeks were thinner than they should have been, and the nose was slightly turned up; but neither defect could disturb so close an approach to perfection. And as for the severe styling of her dress, it only served to define the flatness of her stomach and the fullness of her thighs, and to emphasize, with a sort of sartorial litotes, the fact that her breasts were in blossom.

Christopher Stark turned the photograph over with trembling hands. On the back, a name and address had been written in spidery, unsure letters: *Priscilla Petrovna, Miltonia, Europa.* Yes, he thought, it would have to be Europa, for where else but on Europa did women dress to drive men away? Where else but on Europa was sex synonymous with sin? He had never been there himself, but he had talked with star fishermen who had been. In the heavens of Europa, massive Jupiter brought to mind Hell itself, and as a result, Catholic, Protestant and Jew had merged to found a new Puritanism. It takes a puritanical god to cope with a visible hell, and on the barren plains of Europa the ghosts of John Milton and John Bunyan walked side by side, and woe betided those who crossed their paths.

Standing among the tiny piscine meteors that would someday adorn the hair and dangle from the pierced noses of the women of Earth, New Earth (nee Venus), and Tethys, standing beside the dead man who had robbed him of two-thirds of his catch; standing there in the hold of his robot-brained catamaran, rooted to the steel deck by his magnetic fishing boots, Christopher Stark looked at the photograph of the girl again and knew his destiny. The women in his life, other than those he had bought and paid for, had been few and far between, but there had been enough of them for him to know that the woman whose likeness he stood devouring now was the one for him.

He gazed down at the dead man. Her grandfather, probably; possibly her great grandfather. In either event, Priscilla Petrovna would be beholden to the man who returned him to Europa for a decent burial. He, Christopher Stark, would be that man. Supplies could be obtained on Europa from the N.E.S.N. contingent stationed there—at twice their original price, perhaps, but they could be obtained. And so could fuel. He needed both supplies and fuel, Christopher Stark did, and he needed something else far more. He needed love. He had needed it all his life, and the need had created an emptiness in him that he had been at a loss to understand till now.

He kicked off his boots and slipped out of his tanks and togs; then he ascended the hatch ladder to the galley. From the galley it was but a few steps to the control room. As he stepped through the doorway the port-viewscreen caught his eye, and he stopped in his tracks, momentarily stunned.

He had never seen the constellation before. He had not known, in fact, that such a constellation existed.

The port-viewscreen employed a 100" cathode tube and reduced objects to one-third of their actual size ; and yet it was barely able to frame the star pattern that the port-camera was telecasting. The pattern delineated a macrocosmic star fisherman casting a macrocosmic net.

Compared to him, Orion was a pygmy, Andromeda, a baby girl. The stars of his arms and shoulders ran the gamut from red to blue, from giant to dwarf, from Population I to Population II. His eyes were supernovae, his hair was a cosmic storm. The pale blur of a distant island universe was his navel, and the nebula-pillars of his mighty legs caught and threw back the red-golf radiance of the Centauri trilogy. The net which he had just cast, and which seemingly had ensnared the catamaran, was compounded of a vast sprinkling of nearer stars, and through its interstices showed the coruscating waters of the sea of space.

Overwhelmed by grandeur too great for his mind to grasp, Christopher Stark involuntarily lowered his eyes. When he raised them again, the constellation was gone. And yet the parts that had constituted it still remained. The supernovae that had been the eyes were till there, and so was the cosmic storm that had been the hair. The island universe that had been the navel still pulsed faintly in the immensities, and the nebulae that had been the legs and torso still threw forth their red-gold glare. But now he saw each component out of context with the whole, and try as he would, he could not reattain the perspective that had enabled him to view the over-all design.

Had he really seen the constellation at all? he wondered, as he punched out a destination card for Europa. Or had his unconscious mind created a visual wish-fulfillment fantasy and tied it in with available phenomena? He did no know, and in all probability he never would. But there was one thing that he did know—

The star fisherman had been himself.

To get mid twenty-third century Europa, take away Jest and youthful Jollity, and Sport that wrinkled Care derides. Take away warm sunlight and soft rains. Take away the singing of birds, and the flowers that appear on the earth, and take away the Grape that can with Logic absolute the Two-and-Seventy jarring Sects confute. Now throw a glowing acorn up into the sky and call it Sol. To get Miltonia, scatter a handful of small prefab huts over a frozen slough of despond, and add two large huts, one with a steeple that thrusts like a rusted needle into the brooding sky, the other with four ithyphallic stacks that emit a thick foul-smelling smoke. The hut with the steeple is the Neo-puritan Church, and the hut with the stacks is the factory where omazone, Miltonia's sole *raison d' etre*, is processed. To get Calvinville, Brownsville, Hutchinson's Corners and Bunyantown, repeat the *modus operandi* four times. Now arrange the five villages in a wide circle and place the Europa spaceport in the center. You have only three more props to go—the tower, where a reluctant contingent of the New Earth Space Navy maintains a round-the-clock tour of duty, the barracks where the off-duty personnel sleep, and the fuel house. Place the tower on the perimeter of the port, and dig two nearby holes. Bury the barracks in the first and the fuel house in the second.

Standing in the tower window, Christopher Stark watched the laborious approach of the snow-tractor over the wind drowned plain. Preceding the tractor was a small snow-runabout driven by the messenger whom the tower operator had dispatched to Miltonia with the news that a ship had arrived bearing an unidentified dead man who had been found drifting in the Alpha Centauri Archipelago and who had had in his possession a photograph of Priscilla Petrovna. Upon the wide seat of the tractor sat two women and a man.

Chris waited till the brief caravan had almost reached its destination before he descended the tower stairs to the locks. After swallowing an oxygen tablet, he stepped out into the thin cold air. Despite the bulky parka that all but engulfed her, he identified Priscilla instantly, and it was she to whom he spoke when the tractor grunted to a stop. "I'm Christopher Stark," he said, handing her up the photograph. "I thought perhaps that the man I found might be your grandfather."

She took the photograph from him and gazed at it with green-gold eyes. Looking up at her, Chris drank deeply of her profile. Yes, she was the one, his heart sang. His whole being knew it now.

Presently she slipped the photograph into a pocket of her parka and looked down at him. "Wilt thou show us the body?"

He nodded, and she and the tall dour man who was her father and the short dumpy woman who was her mother climbed down from the seat, followed him into the tower and thence into the first-floor storeroom where the dead man, enshrouded in a tarpaulin, lay upon a makeshift bench. Chris uncovered the face, and the three Petrovnas looked down upon the frozen features for some time. At length Priscilla raised her eyes. "Wouldst thou mind leaving us alone for a moment, Mr. Stark?" she asked.

He went out and stood in the late-afternoon dimness and tried to smoke a cigarette. The oxygen-starved atmosphere thwarted him, and he flung the butt at the sinking acorn-sun. Priscilla appeared at his elbow. "The body is that of my grandfather," she said. "My father's father. My mother's father died when she was still a child." She paused. Then, hesitantly, "Wouldst thou care to accompany us to our humble home and accept our hospitality during thy stay?" she asked. "It will be but small recompense for the service thou hast rendered us, but it is all we have to offer."

"Thank you," Chris said, barely able to control his exultation. Suddenly he gave a start and stared over her shoulder at the horizon. Pale fires were burning all along it, and a ghastly pallor was seeping into the sky.

Turning, Priscilla sought the cause of his consternation. Then, "Do not be alarmed," she said. "It is the planet Jupiter rising."

He watched it rise as he sat in the bed of the tractor beside the dead man on the way to Miltonia. It was in its full-phase and at first it resembled a monstrous, handed mountain emerging from a petrified sea. Then the red spot appeared, and the simile was struck from his mind. No mountain this, but a vengeful Polyphemus with a single flaming orb. The metaphor, however, proved to be as ineffective as the simile. It was as though the heavens had been split asunder to make room for a vast and turbulent mass that was neither sun nor moon nor planet. but the incarnation of Hell, and as though that were not demoralizing enough, the surface of Europa took on. in the dull red radiance, the appearance of the valley of the shadow of death.

The tractor crawled through the shadow, the prayers of the three Petrovnas sounding above the grunting' of the motor. Christopher Stark had never seen Jupiter at such close range before, and the religion which he had inherited from his middle-class parents—a religion compounded of reassuring sayings. Christmas trees, Easter bonnets, turkeys, cranberry sauce, and prosperity, and presided over by a benevolent, all-forgiving god—proved inadequate for the ordeal. On Europa you needed an unbending, eye-for-an-eye god—a god who could fight the devil on the devil's own ground and with the devil's own weapons—and it was as logical as it was inevitable that such a god should have come into being.

The wake lasted seven clays. On Europa, daylight and darkness were practically indistinguishable; nevertheless, the moon's eighteen-hour rotation period had been prorated into three equal portions—morning." afternoon, and night. Mornings, Priscilla's mother sat beside the dead man in the heatless shed that adjoined the Petrovna hut ; afternoons, Priscilla's father sat with him; nights, Priscilla sat with him, and beside her sat Christopher Stark.

An unorthodox courtship. Certainly—but no more unorthodox than it was fruitless. Christopher Stark talked and Priscilla Petrovna listened. He talked of space and stars and fishes, and of the pleasure dome he would someday decree in an as yet undecided upon Xanadu. When these subjects evoked no response, he talked of the book he someday intended to write, and when the book got him nowhere, he sur rendered to the frenzied clawing of his tiger and talked of the women he had known, augmenting their pitiful ranks with many he had not known, and while he did not say outright that all of them had been his for the taking, he broadly implied that such was the case. She gave him a long cold look, and the silence that ensued was even more embarrassing than its predecessors.

Finally, becoming desperate, he came right out and said what he wanted to say. It was the seventh and final night. During the day the temperature had risen slightly above the freezing mark, and the smell of death was in the room. "I realize," he began, "that a wake is a sacred thing, but love is sacred too, and since I'll be leaving tomorrow I think I'm justified in saying now that from the first moment I looked at your picture I've been in—"

Priscilla had risen to her feet. "Dost thou wish a glass of water?" she asked. "I will get thou one," she went on, without waiting for his answer.

When she brought it, he tried to touch her hand. She drew back from him as though he were a leper. Suddenly furious, he seized her arms and pulled her against him. The glass of water fell from her fingers and shattered on the floor. He kissed the curls that peeped from her bonnet He kissed her forehead. He kissed her lips. The stench of the dead man intensified, hovered like malefic vapor in the room.

At last he released her and stepped back. Her face was white, her body rigid. In contrast with her marmoreal aspect, little golden fires were burning in her eyes. He could almost hear the crackling of their tiny flames. "I'm sorry," he said, aghast at what he had done. "Please forgive me."

She turned her back on him without a word and knelt down beside the crude casket in which the dead man lay. Bending her head, she said, "O almighty and vengeful Father, exact what payment Thou must for the apostasy Thou hast witnessed this night, but grant us on the morrow a clement day in order that this, thy wandering pilgrim, who has journeyed home at last, may know the reassuring radiance of Thy sun before his ascent into the maelstrom of Hell. Grant also that he may find the strength to survive the straits of Purgatory, and that he may emerge at last, purified and ennobled, before thy shining gates. Amen."

Christopher Stark tiptoed from the room.

Apparently Priscilla's prayers were answered, for the next day dawned bright and clear—as bright and clear, at any rate, as it was possible for a day to dawn on Europa. The funeral took place in the morning, and in order that the whole village might attend, the omazone processing factory was shut down and work was suspended in the outlying fields, where the lichen-like plant was cultivated. Christopher Stark sat through the grim ceremony in the church and afterward followed the Miltonians to the cemetery. The dour expressions on the faces of adult and child alike matched the lugubrious intonations of the Bunyanesque pastor, but not a single tear was shed when at last the crude casket was lowered into the freshly-dug grave. Indeed, when each of the three Petrovnas cast a handful of snow and ice into the gaping hole, Chris got the impression that whatever sorrow they and the others might be experiencing stemmed not from the burial ceremony itself but from the fact that it was over.

That afternoon Priscilla's father returned to the omazone fields, and she and her mother went back to work in the processing factory. Left alone in the hut, Chris paced the floor in the naked radiance of the unshaded electric-light bulb that hung from the ceiling . He could remain no longer. His catamaran, refueled and re-provisioned, stood waiting for him in its berth, its hold as ravenous for fishes as his billfold was ravenous for the blue-backs that the fishes would bring in. *His* catamaran? No, not really his. Thanks to his prodigality in the New Babylon fun-houses, the back payments that he owed on it were as numerous as the fun-girls he had squandered them on. No, he could not remain—and yet he could not go either. Priscilla Petrovna was a sickness in him now, a sickness that only his having her could cure. The mute which her strait-laced religion had forced her to put upon the trumpet of her sex merely served to make the trumpet blare all the more loudly in his ears.

Would she come with him? he wondered. The unspoken question was so absurd that he almost laughed aloud. No, she would not come with him—not voluntarily, anyway.

He came to a s top in the middle of the floor. The naked light from the bulb above his head elicited every sordid detail of the room: the primitive stone hearth with its incongruous electric fire, the anachronistic iron kettle hanging incongruously over the glowing coils; the severe straight-backed chairs, the mean and narrow windows, the jerry-built ladder leading up into the drafty loft. Would it be a crime to take a woman away from such surroundings? Wouldn't it really be an act of mercy? His catamaran was a three-man job, and the supplies he had taken on would sustain two people for a good six months. Surely in that length of time he ought to be able to win Priscilla's love, and even if he failed and she still hated him enough to press a kidnaping charge against him, it would be her word against his provided—of course, he brought the abduction off in such a way that there would be no witnesses, or that if there were, their testimony would be worthless.

Suddenly he remembered the little hypno-camera he had bought on impulse during his last sojourn in New Babylon. It was an out-and-out gadget devised for no other purpose than the laughs that could be obtained by hypnotizing someone while you snapped his picture; but sometimes a gadget could be a godsend. He got it out of his kit and read the instructions on the back. Then, fingers trembling, he set the hypno-dial for the maximum time-period. Priscilla's department in the omazone factory started work an hour sooner and let out an hour earlier than her mother's, and as for her father, he frequently worked till midnight in the fields. Unless Priscilla refused to have her picture taken, therefore, nothing stood between her and her abduction except the hours that had to elapse before she arrived home.

Chris was half afraid that she would refuse. She did not, however, but posed for him without demur. After that, it was merely a matter of telling her to pack her things, driving her to the spaceport in the snow-tractor, and making sure that the N.E.S.N. man on duty saw her boarding the catamaran seemingly of her own accord. He blasted off just as Hell was rising into the heavens.

The gravity-control center made the proper self-adjustments, and the robot-brain established the catamaran in a suitable orbit around Europa which would be maintained until such time as standard operating procedure should be superseded by specific destination data. Christopher Stark wasted no time in preparing that data, and in feeding it into the time-space nexus-compensator—a mandatory device that eliminated the temporal discrepancies encountered during transphotic velocities. Then, as the catamaran broke orbit and began accelerating, he left the control room and headed for the little cabin where he had left Priscilla.

The hypno-period had worn off some time ago, and he found her lying on the narrow bunk, staring expressionlessly at the ceiling. He paused just inside the door. "I'm sorry I had to trick you," he said. "I'll treat you well, I promise."

She made no answer. She did not even turn her head.

"Look," he said, "you're only making things difficult for both of us. You're here, and there's nothing you can do about it. We're going fishing together, you and I are," he went on warmly. "I've extra gear and togs, and you can help me man my nets, and I'll split the profits with you fifty-fifty. All right?"

The catamaran gave a slight shudder as it hit C-plus velocity, and the cabin door creaked. There was no other sound in the room.

"Look at me!" Christopher Stark said. "I'm not a monster. I'll marry you, if you like. I'll marry you the minute we get back with our catch—I swear I will!"

She rolled over on her side and faced the port bulkhead. She spoke no word. Anger claimed him then, and stepping across the room, he seized her by the shoulder and turned her over. The cheap material of her dress ripped beneath his fingers. "What right have *you* got to set yourself above sex?" he demanded. "Do you know what the product you and your people produce Is used for ? Well I'll tell you what it's used for—it's used to rejuvenate old men ! Omazone, testosterone, and black-water baths—add the three of them together and you get old rakes with young men's faces and young men's physiques on the prowl for girls young enough to be their granddaughters !"

He felt the softness of her naked shoulder beneath his fingers then, and his eyes looked down upon the whiteness of her flesh. Weakness came into his legs, and he sank to his knees beside the bunk. He drew her to him and kissed her on the mouth. She did not resist, she did not even move; she merely lay there limply in his arms. When he released her, she fell back upon the bunk like a life-size rubber doll.

Sickened, he strode from the room. It was his first experience with passive resistance.

It was not his last. There was a Gandhi doll named Priscilla Petrovna on the ship, and when you raised its arms and let go, its arm dropped to its side, and when you kissed its lips, its lips were lifeless, and when you spoke to it, it did not answer; for Gandhi dolls are made of rubber, and rubber dolls can neither feel nor hear nor speak. Neither can they love.

Light years out from the orbital shores of Pluto, Christopher Stark cast his first net and dumped his first catch into the hold. In the months that followed, the hold filled inch by inch, and as the hoard of fishes grew, so too grew Christopher Stark's frustration. A Gandhi doll is not good for a man. Inarticulate, unfeeling, it lies passively in his arms, dead to his desire, indifferent to his want, unresponsive to his love. And no matter how much he may love it, without its love in return he cannot carry his own love beyond a kiss, and the time comes when he cannot carry it even that far. Yet still his love, thwarted and ignored, endures. He is a passionate Adonis burdened with a passive Venus who knows naught of the lists of love and regards the hot encounter as a sin against her strait-laced god. He is a doomed Adonis who will unconsciously seek his own destruction, not because he feels himself incapable of love, but because he is incapable of giving vent to the love he feels. Yet he will never let his Venus go.

Coming into Tethys with his six-months' catch, Christopher Stark opened his Venus' door and said, "I'm locking you in the living quarters while I go to market. The ship will be in drydock for hull-repairs and re-provisioning, but it won't do you any good to scream or pound on the hatch. The drydock personnel won't hear you, and even if they did, and let you out, you wouldn't be permitted to leave the port without a passport. Good by."

Silence.

The slamming of the cabin door.

To get mid twenty-third century Tethys, take away the pensive nun, devout and pure, sober, steadfast, and demure. Take away loneliness and fear. Take away the slough of despond and the valley of the shadow of death. Bring back the Grape that can with Logic absolute the Two-and-Seventy jarring Sects confute, and banish the ghosts of John Milton and John Bunyan from the land. Now throw an even smaller acorn up into the sky and call it Sol, and usher in a Brobdingnagian gem of purest ray serene and call it Saturn. To get New Babylon, blow a trillion-dollar bubble in your macrocosmic pipe and set it down upon the land and cause green grass to grow beneath it and scatter crystalline structures all around. Add streets and laughter, fun-girls and gin; sprinkle liberally with prostitutes and pimps. Sully with a disreputable alley or two, and let the one-hundred dollar bills paid out by the fisheries that ring the port come drifting down like big blue snowflakes. To get the seven other Cities of the Plane, repeat the *modus operandi* seven times.

ROBERT F. YOUNG

After marketing his catch, Christopher Stark headed for Fish Alley. Fish Alley was a long and sinuous snake of a street on which you could buy anything as long as it was in some respect immoral or illegal. You could buy lottery tickets, passports, birth certificates and aphrodisiac gas. You could buy mouth guns, fingernail-blades, stomp-heels, eye-gougers and coffee-flavored strychnine tablets. You could buy dirty pictures, dirty books, dirty comic films, dirty movies and dirty records, and if you wanted to badly enough you could even buy dirty dirt. Most important of all, you could buy *stong*.

Stong was Martian bootleg-wine, but its distinction did not end there. It relegated ordinary wine to the status of sarsaparilla. You didn't get drunk on it, you got crazy on it. You didn't get high on it, you went into orbit on it. It didn't take you out of yourself, it divorced you from yourself. It was the Id's best friend, and in Fish Alley, the Id never had it so good.

Christopher Stark went into the first *stong* bar he came to and ordered a drink and told the barmaid to leave the bottle on the bar. Christopher Stark wasn't worried about going crazy. He was crazy already. Rubber-doll crazy. Gandhi-doll crazy. Passive-resistance crazy. No, he didn't have to worry about *going* crazy.

The first drink washed through him like sunlight after a long rain. The second flung wide the door to spring. The third turned the barmaid, who was fat and scrofulous, into Iphigenia. The fourth turned the barroom, which would have made an appropriate setting for Gorki's *The Lower Depths,* into the Temple of Diana at Ephesus. The fifth turned a pick-me-up girl who was sitting at a nearby table into Diana.

He took the bottle and went over and sat down beside her. " Did you ever hear of a Gandhi Doll?" he asked. "Listen, and I'll tell you about one."

"I know a better place we can talk," Diana said.

"About this Gandhi girl," Chris persisted. "There was this old man drifting in space, see, this old man I caught in my net when I was casting for a school of fishes." Abruptly he struck his fist on the table. Hot tears rolled down his cheeks. "That damned old man," he said. "That damned dirty old man! If it hadn't been for him, I never would have met her."

"Sure, fisher-boy, I understand. Come on, we'll go to my place, and you can tell me all about it."

THE STAR FISHERMAN

The Temple of Diana turned around three times, and Diana doubled. Chris reached out and found one of her four hands. "All right," he said. "Let's get going."

The sordid little room in which he awoke some twelve hours later was reminiscent of Raskolnikov's fictitious garret in ancient St. Petersburg. His head was a raw wound, and Diana was gone. So was his billfold. When he sat up, a fat Tethys cockroach ran down the bedpost, rattled across the filthy floor and disappeared into a hole in the wall.

He went looking for Diana. Thanks to his habit of keeping a few blue-backs in a different pocket from the one in which he carried his billfold, he wasn't quite broke, and by the time he found her he had cancelled out some of the effects of his hangover by means of a well-known traditional therapy. She was sitting in a crowded *stong* bar with her pimp. Only she wasn't Diana any more—she was an old whore with a face like a Roman ruin.

Furious with himself for having picked her up, he strode across the room, seized her purse and dumped its contents on the table. His billfold was not numbered among them. She was so stoned that she didn't even recognize him, and she began to scream. Probably she would have screamed anyway. He grabbed her youthful pomaded pimp and went through his pockets. His fingers came upon a roll of blue-backs, and he confiscated it. The pimp seized his arm. "Thief!" the pimp shouted. "Pickpurse!" He faced the crowd of malcontents, miscreants and misfits that was gathering around the table. "You saw him brice me—are you going to let him get away with it?"

Chris tried to free his arm. The pimp hung on for dear life. The cordon tightened around the table. Chris swung then, connected; in sudden fury, he swung thrice more, then leaped over the prostrate body on the floor and squirmed and twisted his way out into the street. Someone had called the police, and a patrol copter was descending. Instinctively he began to run.

Realizing that he was only attracting attention to himself, he slowed to a brisk walk. If it hadn't been for Priscilla's presence on board his catamaran, he would have returned to the bar and taken a chance all his story. With Priscilla on his hands. however, he did not dare. Keeping her imprisoned for longer than a few days was unthinkable, and if the police did not believe him, and detained him for any length of time, he would have to tell them about her. She could then press a kidnaping charge against him with a vengeance, and if his keeping her under lock and key failed to substantiate it, the hypno-camera with its undeveloped roll of imperishable film, which he had foolishly neglected to jettison, would. No, he could not go back, even though by running away he would lose his right. in the eyes of Tethys law, to be presumed innocent until proven guilty—a handicap that, judging from what he had heard about Tethys courts, would virtually assure his conviction.

After passing through the city locks, he stopped in the drydock office to pay his bill. The visiphone buzzed while the clerk was handing him his receipt. "Yes?" the clerk said, turning on the receiver. The fact that appeared on the screen bespoke authority. So did the voice that crackled on the receiver-mike : "Lieutenant Berrand, New Babylon Police, speaking. We have an alert on a fisherman named Christopher Stark. Do you by any chance have his hip in drydock?"

So they knew his name then! His erstwhile Diana must have taken note of his identification papers before destroying them, and as a result had been able to identify him for the police—though she had undoubtedly done so by proxy. He was out of the office in less than a second, and running toward his ship. "Stop him, someone !" the clerk shouted. "Stop him!"

No one did. The catamaran had been eased out of drydock into an empty berth, and stood ready to go. After closing the outer and inner locks behind him, he glanced at the batten-board to see if the cargo locks were secured, then he turned on the control-room radio and tuned it in to the New Babylon police-band. The charge against him proved to be assault-and-robbery·a charge upon which a newly-enacted interplanetary law imposed a five-year statute of limitations. Perhaps it might t urn out to be a godsend in disguise. For years he had needed a force above and beyond his own will power to keep him away from Tethys, and now fate had provided him with one. Tethys had recently seceded from the Terran Empire and at the moment was so unpopular with Earth and New Earth authorities that it received no co-operation whatsoever in the matter of extradition. Hereafter he would market his catches on New Earth then, and salt away his profits in a reliable bank. New Earth had its cesspools too, and one of the worth of them was the major fishery center, but compared to New Babylon, Nantucket II was a child's garden of verses, and presented very little in the way of temptation to a sophisticated fisherman such as himself. He would frequent its seamy side long enough to procure the new credentials he needed, but that was all.

He was starborne in a matter of minutes, his bridges flaming brightly in the wake of the jets. After the catamaran hit C-plus, he went into the living quarters to see if his Gandhi doll was all right. He looked in the lounge first, but she wasn't there. Next he looked in the galley. She wasn't there either. He saved her cabin till last. Probably she was lying on her bunk, sulking. She wasn't, though. Her bunk was empty. So was her cabin. So, suddenly, was Christopher Stark.

Hours later, the rattling of the hatch cover in the galley aroused him from the stupor into which he had sunk. Investigating, he found that the lock had been broken, and presently he located the discarded crowbar with which the job had been done. Stepping into his cabin, he discovered that the desk drawer in which he kept his petty rash had been forced open and that his petty cash was gone. So he knew, at least, how his Gandhi doll had effected her escape, and how she had obtained the wherewithal with which to bribe her way into New Babylon. What he didn't know was how he was going to endure five long years without her. The drunkard may be aware that he is better off without the drink he craves, but the knowledge will not in any way alleviate his craving.

What does the drunkard do, though, when the drink is removed from the bar and the bar room is shut down for five long years? Answer: if he is wise, he exploits the situation for all it is worth and tries to cure himself.

Thus, in a similar manner, did Christopher Stark try to cure himself of Priscilla Petrovna. He searched first of all for a substitute, and found it partly in the perfecting of his trade and partly in the writing of the book that had been seething in him for years. He no longer fished at random, but pored over map after map of the Trans-solar Sea till he knew the co-ordinates of every fishing bed by heart and could calculate the probable trajectories of the schools for years to come. During the periodic intervals when he put in to Nantucket II to market his ratches and to take on fuel and supplies, he patronized, not bars, but banks and libraries, depositing his profits in the former and assimilating all the information he could find on star- fishing in the latter.

He wrote the book four times before he gained sufficient mastery of the English language to enable him to say what he wanted to say in the way that what he wanted to say should be said. Then, his apprenticeship behind him, he threw away his first four attempts and embarked upon the fifth. At last the words commenced to flow; at last the scenes began to take on depth and color; at last the action broke free from the morass of hackneyed phrases through which it had been laboring and took on wings. He wrote about himself, or thought he did. Actually, his self-image was his hero. But that was all right. Few novelists have the honesty of Stendhal, and even Stendhal was oftentimes remiss when it came to setting himself down on paper. Christopher Stark's protagonist was a star fisherman named Simon Peters. He was tall and broad-shouldered and well-proportioned. He was brilliant, and he was beautiful. He was a demigod, in fact, and in common with most demigods he had an Achilles' heel, and his Achilles' heel was women. He was as much a fisher of females as he was of fishes, and his catches in both categories were legion. In the background loomed the constellation of the Brobdingnagian star fisherman that Chris had glimpsed—ages ago, it seemed now—and over shadowing the action was deep space itself. The title emerged of its own accord: *The Fishes of the Sea.*

When he put in to Nantucket II toward the end of the fourth year, he dispatched the manuscript to a New Boston publishing house and laid over awaiting a reply. He waited for six weeks, a period of time that freed him at last from the assault-and-robbery charge and opened up the gates of New Babylon to him once again. When at last the reply arrived, he was impatient to be gone, more ravenous than ever for his Gandhi doll. The cure had only made more hungry the appetite it had tried to sublimate, and his sickness was now a disease.

But while the cure had failed in one sense, it rewarded him richly in another. The publishing house agreed to publish his book, and when he finally set out for Tethys, his Nantucket II bank account, sizeable to begin with, was even larger, thanks to the advance in royalties he had received. He was thirty-four by then, and the autumn of his youth was past; but Winter still remained, and winter, it was said, was the sweetest season of the lot. He would see.

Before looking for Priscilla, he went to the New Babylon Police Station and turned himself in. Less than an hour later, he was turned back out again with an irate admonition to watch his step and an equally irate warning to the effect that next time Big Brother would be watching, and would clobber him but good. He laughed, and headed for Fish Alley. The date was the first of April, 2253.

This time he did not stop in the first *stong* bar he came to, nor the second, nor the third. Instead he began a systematic tour of the various backroom-agencies that specialized in forged passports. The information he wanted was not easy to come by, but blue-backs have persuasive tongues, and in the sixth backroom he visited, a bent old man dredged up a five-year-old memory of the customer Chris painstakingly described. Yes, she had been there, the old man said. The reason he remembered her was because of her strange clothing. The name she had used? The old man remembered that too, because of its odd flavor. Petrovna, that was it. Prisciila Petrovna. No, she hadn't said anything about leaving New Babylon; to the contrary, the old man had received the impression that she intended to settle down there.

Chris grimaced. He could have saved himself half a hundred blue-backs simply by looking up her name in the New Babylon visiphone directory. He proceeded to do so after leaving F ish Alley. There was only one Petrovna listed—a Miss Priscilla Petrovna. He expelled a breath of relief. She had not married then.

Should he call her? he wondered. He decided not to. Gandhi dolls, for all their listlessness in other matters, were perfectly capable of turning off visiphones. They were capable of closing doors too, but not if you got your foot in first. The address listed in the directory was *209-9 Star Lane*. He could be there in a matter of minutes if he took an anti-grav cab.

He did so. Star Lane was devoted exclusively to modest apartment structures. Ascending the ramp of no. 206, he discovered that he was trembling. He was suddenly furious with himself. Did this little Neopuritan who despised the ground he walked on simply because he had committed a sacrilege in the eyes of her vengeful god mean so much to him that he was going to go on fawning at her feet forever? Self-hatred shook him. He would turn around this very minute and get back to his ship as fast as his legs would carry him and blast off for the Transalar Sea! He went right on ascending the ramp.

At the ninth level, he turned into a narrow corridor and walked down it till he came to a door with her name on it. Still trembling, still despising himself, he pressed his forefinger against the visitor-button . He was almost relieved when the door said, "Miss Petrovna is not at home." "Did she say where she was going?" he asked.

"Yes, said the door. "To her place of employment—six-one-oh Fun Street.

He was dumbfounded. Priscilla working in a *fun-house?* Priscilla a fun-girl? His little Neopuritan Gandhi doll entertaining *men* for a living? He simply couldn't believe it. He didn't believe it, either, till he stepped through the entrance of no. 610 Fun Street and saw her dancing on one of the tables.

It wasn't a particularly risque dance. Nevertheless he was shocked. He was shocked for the simple reason that it was Priscilla who was performing it. He would have been shocked even if she had been standing still. Her being on the table would have been enough in itself to shock him. Her tight, thigh-length dress would have been enough for that matter, not to mention the ring in her nose and her bobbed hair. She didn't have to *dance.*

He stood just within the entrance, incapable for the moment of proceeding another step. Saturn had risen, and showed like a great and shining jewel through the transparent roof. Its argent luminescence, pouring prodigally down into the room, bathed objects and persons alike in a radiance that paralleled the brightness, but not the harshness, of Old Earth sunlight. Watching the subtle inter play of silvery light and slightly darker silvery shadow, he thought he understood why Priscilla had changed.

She had changed because Hell no longer hovered over her head. She had changed because she no longer needed to identify sex with sin. She had changed because she no longer had to walk in the valley of the shadow of death.

He willed himself to step farther into the room, deeper into the jewel-light. She saw him then, and stopped in the middle of her dance. The *avant garde* combo that had been accompanying her movements ceased operations also, and a thunderclap of silence shattered the cacophony. Priscilla put the silence to rout. "Chris!" she cried, leaping down from the table and running across the floor to meet him. "Chris !"

Again he found himself in a state of disbelief. He came out of it with her kisses on his lips. "Chris," she said again, "Chris, Chris ! I've counted the days and the months and the hours. I knew—I hoped, I prayed —that you'd come back!"

They walked hand in hand through the silvery Saturnian rain to her apartment structure. They climbed the ramp side by side, arms swinging, fingers intertwined. He dwelled deep in a dream now, a dream compounded of wonderment and delight. Was this the same Priscilla Petrovna who had sat silently beside him in the heatless little shed on Europa? Was this the languid Gandhi doll who had driven him half out of his mind in the wastes of the Trans-solar Sea? Where were the golden fires of hatred that had once burned so brightly in her eyes? Surely they had not gone out completely.

In her living room, she said, "I've missed you, Chris." In her bedroom, she said, "These are the others."

It was difficult, swimming to the surface of the fathom-deep dream. "The others?" he said, like a golem made of wood. "What others?"

She pointed to a row of snapshots on the wall above her bed. "You know what others," she said.

He leaned across the bed, gripping the headboard to support himself. The snapshots were of men. He did not look at them closely—he knew he would be sick if he did—but he counted them. *Nine*, he counted. *Nine*.

He straightened. For a moment he thought that he was going to faint. Priscilla was regarding him triumphantly, and the golden fires were burning once again in her eyes. *My God, how she must hate me!* he thought. He had known, of course, that there had been other men—her pierced nose had told him that. But to have her flaunt them in his face! To have her use them as a whip with which to flail him! He had not dreamed such hatred could exist.

He staggered from the room. She hurried after him, caught up to him as he was opening the corridor door. "Now that you know, what are you going to do about it, Christopher Stark ?" she said.

ROBERT F. YOUNG

Fury shook him then, and his hands leaped up and gripped her throat. "I'm going to kill you." he heard his hoarse voice say. "I'm going to choke out every last bit of rotten life that's in you !"

She did not move, showed not the slightest sign of fear. She knew as well as he did that his words were empty; that however much she had hurt him, she had not destroyed his love. A man cannot murder a woman because she hates him. He must hate her too—and Christopher Stark found himself wanting in the balance.

His hands fell away, and be ran from the room. He ran along the corridor and down the ramp to the street. In the street, he almost collided with a woman who was turning in toward the apartment-structure entrance. He slowed to a walk then. He walked and walked. The silvery rain of sinking Saturn faded out and disappeared. The street lights came on. He continued to walk. After a while his foot steps took on direction, and at length he found himself passing through the New Babylon locks and out into the spaceport. Immediately his limbs grew heavy, and out of force of habit he slipped an oxygen tablet into his mouth. He saw the two New Babylon police officers then, out of the corner of his eye. They had just emerged from the locks and were hurrying toward him. He paused and stood there waiting for them to come up, idly wondering what they wanted, but not caring very much. One of them he noted absently, had a hypnogun in his hand. Now he was pointing it; now there was a kaleidoscope whirling before Christopher Stark's eyes. "I'm arresting you for the murder of Priscilla Petrovna," said the officer with the gun. "Yes sir," said Christopher Stark mechanically, and accompanied the two officers back to the city.

*

Name of victim : Priscilla Petrovna
Time and date of death : 5 :23-5:34 P.M. 1st April, 2253, N.E.S. time
Scene of death : no. 206-9 Star Lane, New Babylon, Tethys
Cause of death: strangulation
Murder weapon: a pair of hands
Witnesses: (1) apartment no. 9 responsi-portal; (2) Sarah Bennett

THE STAR FISHERMAN

Remarks: The accused insisted, despite the presence of his fingerprints both upon the deceased's throat and in her bedroom, and despite the testimony of the responsi-portal, the memory banks of which recorded his very words ("I'm going to kill you. I'm going to choke out every last bit of rotten life that's in you."), and the testimony of Sarah Bennett, who saw him running out of the apartment structure at approximately 5:25 P.M. on the afternoon of the murder, that he was deeply in love with the deceased and would have been incapable of strangling her. The accused's past record, however, suggested strongly that he was prone to violence, and the consuming love which he admitted feeling toward the deceased when weighed against the snapshots which he admitted seeing in her bedroom left so little doubt as to his guilt that the court refused to permit an investigation of the subjects of the snapshots on the grounds that such a procedure would impugn their reputations without serving any purpose.

Name of the accused: Christopher Stark

Occupation: star fisherman

*

They sentenced him to forty years in the penal colony on Deimos. Compared to Deimos, the island of Alcatraz is a pleasant Pacific atoll. Deimos is a true rock. According to Martian folklore, it is one of the two mountains which the giant Felikannibub tore up by their roots in a fit of anger and threw at the sun. It is unfortunate that he did not throw it hard enough for it to attain an escape velocity beyond that required for an orbit, for the Martian sky would be much better off without it. It is ugly and misshapen, and about as inspirational to look at as an old shoe.

The penal colony which the good folk of Tethys built for the chastisement of their major criminals has long since degenerated into a ruin. It had something of the aspect of a ruin in Christopher Stark's day. The prison proper was built of huge stone blocks, and encircled a bleak area euphemistically called an exercise enclosure. The pursuits of the prisoners were twofold: walking in the enclosure and sleeping in their cells. In addition, there was a third, optional, pursuit: thinking. And therein lay the rack, the screw, the whipping post; therein lay the price that the prisoner paid for his crime against his fellow man. Therein lay insanity.

ROBERT F. YOUNG

Unless, like Christopher Stark, he could give his thinking direction. Unless, like Christopher Stark, he had a murder to erase. Unless, like Christopher Stark, he was determined to see his true love once again.

After serving his sentence, Christopher Stark would be seventy-four years old. He would, if he were lucky, have ten more years to go. How best to spend those years? How best to bet their days and weeks and months so that when at last Death took his hand it would not find him with an empty purse? Night after lonely night, Christopher Stark lay awake in his bunk, staring up through his cell window at the orange expanse of Mars, pondering the question. And all the while he knew the answer. For if there had been two Priscillas, there had to be a third. The Neo-puritan Priscilla represented one apogee of the arc of the pendulum, and the fun-girl Priscilla, the other. In between the two apogees there had to be a Priscilla who combined the two extremes, who was half Neopuritan and half fun-girl ; who was the sort of woman, in short, whom the average man falls in love with and marries. This was the Priscilla he would pursue next, and in the process change the past and erase her murder.

A large order, to be sure; but *The Fishes of the Sea* had become a phenomenal best-seller, and Christopher Stark was rich. Not as rich as Croesus, perhaps, but rich enough, nevertheless, to buy quite a number of things. And so he lay on his bunk, night after night , and looked up through his cell window into yesterday. And Deimos spun upon its orbit in the vast and complex Grandfather's clock of space, and Mars turned and the Earth turned, and the solar system crept imperceptibly along upon its journey within a journey, and the Milky Way Galaxy pinwheeled lazily as it traveled with its sisters NGC 147, TGC 185, NGC 205, NGC 221, NGC 278, NGC 404, GC 598, and M 31 toward a destination man would never know, and eventually one trillionth of a cosmic second passed, and forty years went down the drain of time.

The sign on the frosted door said, HICKMAN REJUVENATION CENTER, *New Earth Banch.* The old man who had just stepped off the elevator opened the door and went in. "I have an appointment with Dr. Hickman," he told the girl behind the outer-office desk. "My name is Christopher Stark."

THE STAR FISHERMAN

The girl gave him a glance that was both knowing and contemptuous, then nodded in the direction of the inner-office door. "You may go in now," she said.

Dr. Hickman was a wiry little man with bright brown eyes and wispy brown hair. He stood up when Chris entered and shook hands. "Won't you sit down, Mr. Stark?"

Chris did so. "First of all," he said, "I want to know how many years I'll lose."

Dr. Hickman leaned forward. "But first of all, Mr. Stark. I must know how old—or rather, how young—you want to be."

"Twenty-five," Chris said.

"H'm'm."

" I'll want a different face too something a little more pleasing to the eye than the one I've got. and varied enough so that I won't be recognized. Also, I'll want broader shoulders, and about two more inches of height. Can you take care of all that too ?"

"Oh yes," Dr. Hickman said. "It's part of our regular service. How old are you now?"

"Seventy-four," Stark answered.

"I see." Dr. Hickman got a glossy booklet out of his desk, riffled through it to the page he wanted and ran a forefinger down two parallel columns of figures. Presently his bright brown eyes flicked upward. "Assuming you're in reasonably good health. ten years will get you two, Mr. Stark."

Chris nodded. He had hoped for three, but beggars can't be choosers, even when they're rich. "How long will it take?"

"Three months-possibly four." Dr. Hickman cleared his throat. "I feel ethically compelled to point out, however," he went on in a more serious tone of voice, "that we do not advise five-to-one speedups. There is always the danger, toward the end, of an acceleration of cellular breakdown, accompanied by rapid synaptic deterioration and—"

Chris interrupted him. "I'll take my chances—just give me the two years. Now, how soon can I begin?"

Dr. Hickman sighed. "Right away, if you like."

"Good," Christopher Stark said. "I'm sick of being an old man."

ROBERT F. YOUNG

*

The sign on the battered door said. V. WESTON. ELECTRONICS EXPERT. *Specialist in ganglion-circuit repairwork.* The tall broad-shouldered young man with the old-looking eyes who had just alighted from the Nantucket II anti-grav cab opened the door and went in. A middle-aged man with thinning hair and a tired face stood behind a tool-cluttered table that functioned as both counter and workbench. "V. Weston?" the visitor asked.

The middle-aged man nodded. "Yes sir."

"I'm Simon Peters," the tall man said. Then, "What do you know about time-space nexus-compensators? Weston's voice was eager.

"Why, I know everything there is to know about them. I can take them apart and put them back together blindfolded. I can—"

"Good," Simon Peters said. "I have one I want you to take apart. It's on a small ketch I just bought. Only when you put it back together, I want you to alter its mechanism in such a way that I can set it for any point in space-time I choose, whereupon it will plot a course containing the necessary spatial distance and synchronize that distance with the requisite transphotic velocity and bring the ship to the chosen point in a matter of hours. Can you do it ?"

V. Weston had paled. "Yes, I can do it, Mr. Peters. That's not the point. Surely you must be familiar with the nexus-statute of the interplanetary code."

"I certainly am," said Simon Peters. "So familiar with it, in fact, that I can recite it word for word. 'Any person convicted of willfully tampering with a time-space nexus-compensator shall be liable to not more than twenty-five years in prison and not less than ten, and any person convicted of deliberately altering a time-space nexus-compensator for the purpose of retro-travel shall be liable to the death penalty'. They'll tell you, Mr. Weston, that the past belongs to the people who lived in it, and that we of today are ethically bound to stay out of it; but what they won't tell you is that they're afraid of someone going back to a previous era and amassing a fortune through his foreknowledge, thereby instituting a financial chain of events that could conceivably make the poor of today rich, and the rich of today poor. So you see, Mr. Weston, retro-travel isn't ethically wrong—it's merely financially hazardous to the powers-that-be."

Weston's accelerated blink rate indicated that the point had gotten home. However, he was not won over yet. "The penalty is still death, Mr. Peters," he said.

"Look," Simon Peters said. "I don't know whether I can change the past. I think—I hope—I can, in a very small way. But even if I do, and future events *are* altered, no one can possibly be aware of the fact. So if you're apprehended, Mr. Weston, it won't be because of anything I do—or have done—in the past. Ships disappear every year, and for all we know, they and their owners make the journey into yesterday ; but I have never heard of anyone being convicted, or even accused, of gimmicking a time-space nexus-compensator. So all you've really got to worry about is how much I'll pay you for the job, and you don't really have to worry about that, because I'll pay you any price you ask. What do you say, Mr. "Veston?"

Some of the tiredness departed from Weston's face, and he stood up a little straighter. "I'm sick of being poor," he said.

"Good," said Simon Peters. "Come on, I'll take you to my ketch."

*

He chose the date carefully. The rejuvenation center had guaranteed him two years, but he could afford to take no chances; hence he allowed two weeks leeway, and emerged in the Tethys stratosphere on the fifteenth day of April, 2251, one year, eleven months and two weeks before the day Christopher Stark would walk out of Priscilla Petrovna's apartment to be—or not to be accused of her murder.

After berthing his ship, he entered New Babylon. He tried Fun Street first, gambling that his true love had already embarked upon her career. The gamble paid off: he found her in the same house Christopher Stark would find her one year, eleven months and two weeks hence.

She was sitting at a corner table, all alone. Her tawny hair, as yet unbobbed, rippled to her shoulders. Her cheeks were fuller than they had been in Miltonia, and the sternness of her mouth and chin was less severe. He went over and sat down beside her. "You're new here, aren't you?" he said.

ROBERT F. YOUNG

She gave a start when she first looked at him, and for a moment he thought she had recognized him. Apparently, however, she had not, for she merely said, "Not really new. I've been here almost a month. After working for three years in a dress shop to raise my bond, it seems like heaven."

"Oh, then you're not so new at that. My name is Simon Peters."

"Priscilla—Priscilla Petrovna."

"Will you dance with me?" She nodded brightly, and stood up. The *avant garde* combo was not in evidence, and subdued music was emanating from hidden speakers. The edge of Saturn's outer ring was just beginning to show through the transparent roof. Seeing her again had nearly torn him apart. Dancing with her did. He held her tightly against him so that she would not notice the tears running down his cheeks, and as soon as the opportunity presented itself, he covertly wiped his eyes. The floor was nearly deserted, and no one witnessed his distress.

He remained with her till her tour of duty was up, then he walked through the New Babylon streets with her to the apartment structure where she lived. It was the same one in "which she would be living when Christopher Stark appeared upon the scene. Was the wall above her bed as yet unsullied with the snapshots that would one day hang there, Simon Peters wondered, or had the deplorable display already been begun ? Her nose was as yet unpierced- true; but the wearing of nose-rings was a custom, not a law, and an unpierced nose was not an infallible sign of virginity. The little-girl kiss she bestowed upon his cheek when they said good night reassured him, and he hummed softly to himself as he walked the streets in search of a suitable place to live.

He began seeing her every day. She did not seem to mind. He bought her stoles and gowns and underthings, and fishes for her hair. But the love he sought did not materialize in her eyes, and while her kisses were remote from the Gandhi-doll kisses he had known on the Trans-solar Sea, they were remote too from the kisses which a woman bestows upon the lips of the man she loves. Small wonder, then, that he should have been surprised when, several months after he first began courting her, she asked him if she could be his mistress.

They were dancing at the time. "You know the answer without asking," he aid, when at last his astonishment abated. "You knew it when I first came over and sat beside you."

"Yes," she said, "I suppose I did. It's funny, isn't it, how two people can just look into one another's eyes and tell."

"Yes," he said, looking into her eyes and not finding the love that should have been there. "Why don't you ask me to marry you while you're at it?" he asked. "I might say yes."

She was startled. "Marry you? Oh, I couldn't do that. You see—"

"Yes?" he said.

"Nothing. It's just that I don't want to get married—not just yet, anyway. Shall we go now?"

"I'll get your coat," he said above the pounding of his heart.

The next day he went with her while she had her nose pierced, and afterward he bought her the most expensive nose-ring he could find. His heart sang while he supervised the selection of a fish-pendant that would do justice to the brightness of her eyes. He had been her first lover after all, he, Simon Peters had. He, Simon Peters, nee Christopher Stark.

Some of his euphoria departed when she bought a small camera and insisted on snapping his picture. Was time mocking him? Was he merely initiating the series of lovers that he was trying to avert? Had his snapshot been one of the nine Christopher Stark had seen—would see—upon the wall above her bed? He looked for it that night, but did not find it. Nor the next night, nor the next. Some of his uneasiness departed then, and as the months passed and the wall remained empty, his fears gradually went away.

But not for long. Although she was his mistress, Priscilla would neither move in with him nor permit him to move in with her. Neither would she permit him to visit her every single night, maintaining that if she did, he might grow tired of her. Consequently, since he did not dare to show himself too often in public places for fear of being identified as Christopher Stark and apprehended for the assault-and-robbery charge, much of his time was relegated to brooding in the little out-of-the-way room he had rented. The inspiration for his brooding, however, arose, not from misgivings concerning

his growing tired of Priscilla, but from misgivings concerning Priscilla's g
rowing tired of him.

As time passed, he began to suspect her of having another lover. Not because of any direct evidence, but because of the flowering of young womanhood that was taking place within her. He was sure that he himself was not the cause of the expectant light that came with ever-growing frequency into her gold-green eyes, the smiles that danced with ever-increasing abandon on her lips, and the happiness that gave her face an ever-greater radiance; and if he was not the cause, then someone else was, and that someone had to be someone she loved.

Perhaps he had eliminated all of her lovers save one. Still and all, though, that one could very well be the one who had made-or who would make—the attempt on her life.

He would see—and soon, too. Much too soon.

*

In settling for two years, he had had in mind two years in a young man's life. The rejuvenation center had given him a young-man's body, but it had not given him a young-man's mind. As a result, he had retained an old-man's perspective of time, and two years to a man of seventy-four is a giddy toboggan ride down an ever icier slope. In Simon Peter's case, the finish-line lay in the valley of the shadow of death.

As the landscape of the days and weeks and months flashed past, harbingers of that finish-line began to appear. His step lost its lightness, his breath grew short; his vision dimmed and his hearing began to fail. And yet no visible evidence of his imminent crossing manifested itself. He was still ostensibly young, still ostensibly healthy; no lines marred his handsome face, and his eyes seemed bright and clear.

But he was dying, and he knew it, and sometimes when he awoke during the night and could not fall back to sleep, he buried his head on Priscilla's breast and clung to her like a frightened child. And if she was not there, and the bed turned out to be his own, he buried his head in his pillow, and cried. And slowly, ineluctably, his time ran out.

*

THE STAR FISHERMAN

On the afternoon of the first of April, 2253, Simon Peters was standing in the shadows behind the *avant garde* combo when Christopher Stark came into the fun-house. Christopher Stark did not see him. Christopher Stark saw no one except the girl dancing on the table.

Simon Peters followed them when they left. After they entered no. 206 Star Lane, he took up a position just to the right of the entrance. He was taken aback when Christopher Stark came running out right on schedule. He had hoped that by eliminating the snapshots he had altered the scheme of things at least a little bit. He hurried into the building just as Christopher Stark nearly collided with Sarah Bennett. Neither of them saw him, and he met no one on the ramp. He was breathing hard when he reached the ninth level, and he had to stop to rest. Glancing at his watch, he saw that the time was 5 :27 P.M. He would have to hurry: her would-be murderer might be in the apartment already. Gripping the hypno-gun which he had bought that morning and which he carried in his right-hand coat-pocket, he hurried down the corridor.

Her door was ajar. Without pausing, he pushed it all the way open and stepped inside. Priscilla was standing in the living room, an expression on her face that he had never seen there before. She started when he entered; then disappointment came into her eyes. "Oh, it's you," she said.

Ignoring her, he walked across the room and stepped into the kitchen. There was no one there. Next, he went into the bedroom. There was no one there either.

Good, he thought. He would be there waiting when her murderer arrived.

He saw the snapshots then. On the wall above her bed. He advanced across the room, leaned across the familiar bedspread.

He counted them. *Nine*, he counted. *Nine*. The first one was strikingly familiar. Peering closer, he saw that it was the snapshot she had taken of him.

She had followed him into the room. "Simon, what's come over you—" she began. And then, her gaze joining his, "Oh, you've seen them. I didn't mean for you to."

"Your lovers, no doubt," he said, confronting her.

"Not, not really—except for the first. For you. The others are men I let pick me up in the street and take me home. I never saw any of them afterward.

34

You see, one would not have been enough." She reached out and touched his cheek in a gesture that came close to being tender. "Poor Simon," she said. "I did not mean to hurt you too."

He could feel the muscles of his face contracting, and there was a throbbing in his forehead. "Who did you mean to hurt?"

She sighed. "Listen, and I will try to explain. On Europa, where I used to live, a man came to us bearing a dead man he thought to be my grandfather. On Europa, the people are desperately unhappy, and when people are desperately unhappy they can find relief in only one way—by exploiting someone who is worse off than they are. Bringing a Europan girl a dead man is like bringing a New Earth girl a box of candy. She will not refuse it, even if it does not rightfully belong to her. Her parents would not let her, and neither would the people of her village. No, she will claim it—and if she is human, she will develop a tender spot in her heart for the man who brought it. In my case, I did not need to. I—I fell in love with him the minute I saw him—so much in love that I feared to speak lest I betrayed myself."

Simon Peters looked at the snapshots on the wall. His voice cracked when he said, "Go on."

"Oh yes," she said, "the snapshots. The-the other men." He looked at her then, and saw the golden fires burning brightly in her eyes, the golden fires that he had once thought to be fires of hatred but which he now knew to be fires of love. "He threw the women he had had in my face, this man did," Priscilla went on, "and now I have thrown the men I have had in his. Now the score is even . For five years I planned and waited for the moment he would return. Now he has run away again, this time to nurse his wounds; but he'll be back. He'll be back because he cannot help himself, because he loves me as much as I love him. Do you know what it's like, Simon, to love someone so much it makes you sick inside?" she asked. "That is how I love this man. And do you know what it's like to love someone that much and yet not be able to indulge your love because the punishment has not yet been exacted? Do you know what it is like to worship the ground someone walks on, and have the ground forbidden to you? Do you, Simon? Do You ?"

He realized a long while later that it was her slender throat that his hands were gripping, that it was her tender flesh into which his furious fingers had dug. He released her then, and she slipped limply to the floor and lay there staring sightlessly at the ceiling. All he could think of was a rubber doll.

*

There were the *stong* bars. After reaching Fish Alley, he stopped in the first one he came to and ordered a drink and told the barmaid to leave the bottle on the bar. It was the way it had been the last time, almost. This time, though, the room didn't turn into the Temple of Diana at Ephesus. It turned int o a long, doorless corridor with blood-red walls. At the end of it a huge idol sat upon an obsidian throne. He walked down the corridor slowly, stumbling now and then. The idol's hair was tawny in hue, and consisted of tiny metallic snakes. Her eyes were green-gold agates. Her black dress was pulled above her knees, and her white-brimmed bonnet was pushed back from her forehead . The front of her dress was open, and one of her marble breasts hung out. A sacrifice had just been performed on the altar that stood before her throne, and she was frozen in the act of plucking an object out of the victim's face. The victim was Christopher Stark, and the object was an eye. Simon Peters threw the bottle he was carrying at her, and collapsed unconscious to the floor.

The dark alley in which he awoke smelled of sewer gas. His billfold was gone, and so was his hypno gun and his watch. His head was throbbing. He got to his feet after a while, and staggered into the street. His chest bubbled when he breathed, and his legs would barely support him. For some reason his trousers were too long for him, and he kept tripping on the cuffs. An eternity passed before he reached the city-locks, another, before he finally gained his ketch.

He blasted off without delay, and set the time-space nexus-compensator for his final destination. With a little luck he could still upset the apple cart of time. With a little luck he could, by altering a single moment, change his entire life. *Begone.* he would say to young Chris Stark. *Cast your net in safer waters!* Right now, though, he was tired. Right now he would sleep.

He retired to his small cabin and collapsed upon the bunk. The shuddering of the ketch as it came out of transphotic awakened him. "Priscilla," he murmured, and eyes still closed. reached out for her beloved body. His hands found nothing but twisted sheets and emptiness, and at last, with horrible abruptness, the realization that she was dead and that he had killed her got through to him. His anguish was unendurable. He got up and fumbled among his belongings for some token, some sign, that she had not ceased to be, some remnant of her that would drive the shadow of her death into a dark corner of the room; and he found, finally, the little hypno-camera with its undeveloped roll of imperishable film. He was as excited as a little child, and like a little child, he got his developing kit and sat down in the middle of the floor and began to play. The picture came out perfectly. She was so lovely that he wanted to cry. He covered her image with kisses, and turned the photograph over and wrote her name and address on the back. *Priscilla Petrovna,* he wrote. *Miltonia, Europa.*

A bell began to ring. Thrusting the photograph into his pocket, he went to investigate. It was the bob-bell: a school of fishes was approaching the catamaran—it was time to get into his togs and tanks. After reversing the ship's direction and adjusting it to a speed just beneath average meteor-velocity, he hurried down into the hold. He wondered what made him so weak. His legs felt like broomsticks, his arms, like pipestems. His hands had atrophied into shriveled claws. A phrase came out of the thickening forest of his memory and trailed through the murky clearing of his mind —*an acceleration in cellular breakdown, accompanied by rapid synaptic deterioration.* He shook his head. The words were meaningless to him. Opening the locker, he took out one of the spacesuits and struggled into it. He could not find his net. No matter. He would reach forth and snare the fishes with his hands. "For you, Priscilla," he whispered, "for you," and activated the locks and stepped through them–into space.

Ketches have no outer decks. Nor are ketch-spaceboots magnetized. Ketches are not catamarans, never were and never will be.

Thus Simon Peters, nee Christopher Stark, torn by his own impetuosity from the gravitic pull of his hurtling craft, went into free fall in the Alpha Centauri Archipelago where he had thought in his naivete to rip out a single stitch in the cosmic hem of time. As he fell, Death reached out and touched his hand, and he pulled his hand away. "No," he said, "not yet—I do not yet know who I am." At his feet lay the red-gold billiard ball of Alpha Centauri. At his elbow, a pale planet poised. Coldness came and grew within him, and

THE STAR FISHERMAN

as the coldness grew, so too grew Christopher Stark. The red-gold sun diminished, and the pale planet waned; the whisperings of the immensities sounded faintly in his ears. He looked forth upon creation with supernovae-eyes and breathed deeply of the abysmal darkness of the night. There was still time for one more cast. The myriad stars of his macrocosmic net rustled as he unfurled it, and the stellar sinews of his Brobdingnagian arm grew taut. Back, back now, the shoulders slanting, now turn and slowly turn, the arm rising. the arm of star, of giants and dwarfs and little motes of dust that micro-men call worlds; the star-arm rising and the star-net swinging wide; now out, now down, the stars he thought, the stars that are my genes, my chromosomes, my corpuscles, my strength, my life, my death and my undoing, the white stars and the blues, the reds, the flaming yellows—I am all—all am I, Christopher Stark, immensities am I, global cluster s and cosmic storms; nebulae and Pleiades and island universes; I am the stars and space, I am the star fisherman in all the coruscating glory of his youth . . . and he swung his great and glittering arm and cast his net—

And snared himself.